Magnet magic

You will need: tissue paper; a recorder; a magnet; an adhesive tab; a basket; a thumb tack.

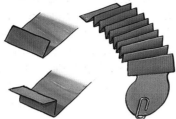

1. Cut a strip of tissue paper 1½ times the depth of your basket to make a snake. Snip one end into an oval for the head and pleat the rest. Slide a paper clip onto the nose and tape it on.

2. Pin the tail to the bottom of the basket with the tack. Now attach a magnet underneath the end of the recorder with an adhesive tab.

3. Hold the recorder above the snake's head. The magnet will pull the paper clip towards it until the snake is fully stretched. Hold the recorder just above the head so the snake hovers and dances as you play.

Don't make your snake too long.

Magnetic wallet

You will need: a 26 x 10cm (10 x 4in) piece of material; four round magnets with holes; needle, thread.

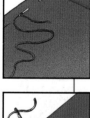

Lay the material face-down. Fold up one short end by 10cm (4in). Pin, then sew along both doubled sides.

Sew two magnets to the pocket and two to the flap so they meet and stick when you fold the flap.

Magnets only stick together one way. Test before you sew. If they don't stick, turn one magnet over. Find out why on page 6.

Decorate with felt stars.

3

Downhill skier

You will need: a piece of cardboard about 40 x 17cm (17 x 8in); playdough; toothpicks; bright paper; self-hardening clay; cardboard; paint; scissors; two paper clips; glue stick; ruler; magnet.

1. Fold back 7cm (3in) of the cardboard and then open it out again. Prop up the flap you have made so the cardboard forms a slope. Paint the slope, if you like.

2. Snip both ends off the toothpicks with a sharp pair of scissors. Put a lump of playdough on the end of each stick and press them onto the slope.

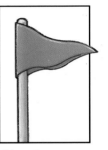

3. Fold a piece of bright paper in half. Draw and cut out triangles on the fold to make flags. Glue each one on the inside. Fold over the top of a toothpick and press.

These bushes are made from sponge painted green.

Spray snow was put on the slope for more realism.

Skier

1. Roll a ball of clay for the head. Form the body, legs and arms and stick them together. The skier should be about 5cm (2in) tall. Cut out cardboard skis, about 5cm (2in) long.

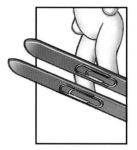

2. Glue a paper clip onto the bottom of each ski. Then glue the skier to the skis. Leave the clay to dry (look at the manufacturer's instructions). Then paint your figure.

To play

Tape a magnet onto a ruler. Then place the skier on top of your slope. Slide the ruler under the cardboard so the magnet attracts the skier's paper clips. Now, using the ruler, guide the skier in and out of the flags. You could time how long it takes to do the run or make two slopes and skiers and have a competition with a friend.

Racing boats

You will need: corks; paper clips; toothpicks; bright paper; playdough; plastic tray; 2 magnets; 2 rulers; books; tape.

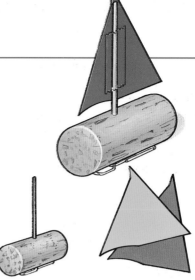

1. Unbend one end of a paper clip. Push it into one side of a cork and a tooth-pick into the other side.

2. Cut out a small triangle from bright paper and stick it to the toothpick for a sail. Make two of these boats.

Cut ends off sticks.

3. Make buoys to sail the boats around. Push a toothpick into a lump of playdough.

4. Cut out and glue paper flags to the sticks (see skier, step 3). Make three of these. Press them onto the tray.

Racing your boats

Put the tray on two piles of books, making sure it is level. Pour in water until it is about 3cm (1½in) deep. Float the boats. Tape a magnet to the end of the ruler. Hold the ruler under the tray and sail the boats around the buoys as fast as you can.

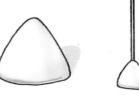

Hovering bee

You will need: a box with one open side (cut away any flaps or use a shoe box); stiff, bright paper; two round magnets (you need ones with a hole in the middle); a needle and thread; scissors; a self-adhesive tab or double-sided tape; glue stick; a piece of bright tissue paper; tape; white, black and yellow pipe cleaners and an extra piece of pipe cleaner for the top of the box.

The box

1. Glue green paper inside one short side of the box and blue paper to all the other sides. Stand the box with the green side at the bottom.

2. Cut out a long, green curved strip and glue it to all the sides around the green base. You could add a cloud, sun and flowers (see right).

Poles apart

Place two magnets together and see what they do. Do they stick together or push apart? Every magnet has a north-seeking and a south-seeking pole. If you put the same poles of two magnets together they will repel each other and push apart.

Like poles repel.

Unlike poles attract.

The bee's magnet will keep pushing away from the magnet underneath to make the bee hover busily over the flower.

6

Bee and flower

1. Bend white pipe cleaners into wings. Wind the ends around the magnet. Wrap around black and yellow pipe cleaners for the bee's body.

2. Try the other magnet under the bee to see which side pushes the bee away. This means the same poles are facing (see left). Mark the top.

3. Put the magnet on a piece of tissue paper, marked side down. Wrap the paper around the magnet and tape. Turn it over and glue on a yellow circle.

Adding to the scene

Draw and cut out flowers, grass, a sun and clouds for your garden scene.

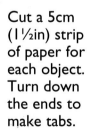

Tabs

Cut a 5cm (1½in) strip of paper for each object. Turn down the ends to make tabs.

Glue one tab onto the picture and the other onto the box.

Draw around a cup.

4. Cut a circle from bright paper. Draw on and cut out petals. Glue to the bottom of the box. Press on the magnet with a self-adhesive tab.

5. Thread a needle and push it up between the bee body's pipe cleaners. Pull it through and knot it so that the bee hangs from the thread.

6. Make a hole in the top of the box and push the needle through. Adjust the thread so the magnets repel and the bee hovers over the flower.

7. Cut a short piece of pipe cleaner to hold the thread. Take the needle off. Wind the thread around the pipe cleaner and knot it.

Shove frog

You will need: a box lid (a shoe box lid will do); paint; white paper; glue; cardboard; a paper clip; 6 small magnets; tape.

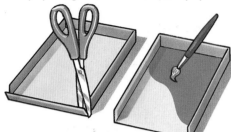

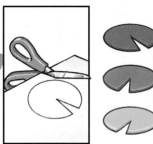

Magnets can attract metal through cardboard and other things.

1. Cut off one of the narrow sides of the lid, as shown. Paint the inside of the lid blue. Leave it to dry.

2. Draw six lily pad shapes on white paper and cut them out. Paint three yellow, two green and one red. Leave to dry.

Glue lily pads on, as shown here.

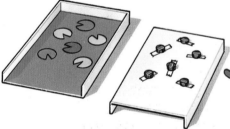

3. Glue the lily pads onto the blue box lid. Turn over the lid and tape one of the magnets under each lily pad.

4. Draw, then paint, a frog shape on some carboard. When dry, cut it out and tape a paper clip underneath.

Playing shove frog

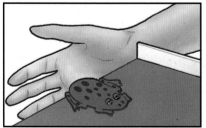

Scoring

Score two points.

Score three points.

Score four points.

To shove, place the frog half on and half off the box, as shown. With the palm of your hand shove it onto the board. The magnets underneath will attract the frog's paperclip.

Take turns to play. On each turn you get three shoves. The way you play the game is to make the frog land on one red, one yellow and one green lily pad each turn.

You score different points for each lily pad you land on: two for yellow, three for green and four for red. So the most you can score in one turn is nine.

Rest the lid on something to make it slope backwards.

Fishing game

You will need: silver foil; paperclips; a small magnet; string; straws; a bowl.

Cut some fish out of silver foil and slide a paper clip onto each of them.

Tie a magnet onto a straw with string. Keep it in place with tape. Make one of these fishing rods for each player.

Put the fish in a bowl of water. Fish for them with the magnet rods. See who can catch the most.

You score four.

You score two.

Your opponent scores two.

You score three.

Your opponent scores three.

Your opponent scores three more.

If you land on two pads the same, you only get points once. Your opponent gets the others. In this example, you get four (red) plus two (one of the yellows) only.

If all three shoves land on the same pads, green for example, you only score once. The points for the two others go to your opponent. As shown above, you only score three.

Batteries and circuits

You will need: 4.5v battery; small screwdriver; 2.5v or 3.5v torch/flashlight bulb; bulb holder; wire - miniature stranded wire is good for making circuits; cardboard; paper clip; 2 paper fasteners.

Making a circuit

1. Cut two pieces of wire and strip both ends of each (see page 32). Put the end of the screwdriver in one of the bulb holder screws. Turn it a few times to loosen the screw but don't take the screw out.

2. Undo the other screw in the same way. Make small loops at the end of the two pieces of wire. Hook a loop around each screw. Wrap the wire around the screw in a clockwise direction.

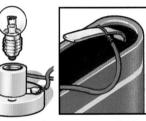

3. Do up both screws tightly with the screwdriver. Screw in the bulb. Bend the free ends of the wires on the bulb holder and wind one onto each battery terminal. The bulb will light up.

If there is a break in the circuit the bulb will not light up.

How it works

The electricity can only flow if it can get from one terminal of the battery to the other. The path it flows through is called a circuit and the electricity that passes through the circuit is called current. One terminal on the battery is positive and one is negative. This is shown by a + sign for positive and a - sign for negative.

Series circuits

Try linking up two bulb holders to the battery as shown here. You will need another piece of wire too. If you remove one of the bulbs, the other goes out. This is because the circuit is broken and the current cannot flow. It is called a series circuit.

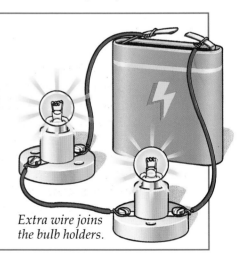

Extra wire joins the bulb holders.

Adding a switch

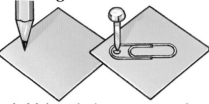

1. Make a hole in a piece of cardboard with a sharp pencil. Hold one end of the paper clip over the hole and push a paper fastener through. Bend back its prongs underneath.

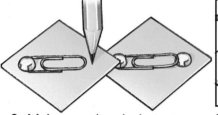

2. Make another hole just outside the other end of the paper clip and push a paper fastener through. Bend back the prongs but do not let them touch the first paper fastener at the back.

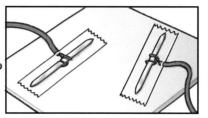

3. Cut two wires and strip the ends. Turn over your switch and wind one end of each wire to each paper fastener. Tape over the prongs at the back with insulating tape.

4. Join one wire to a bulb holder and wind the other wire onto a battery terminal. Cut a new piece of wire and attach one end to the second battery terminal and the other end to the bulb holder.

Parallel circuits

Join a wire to each terminal. Twist two short wires onto the free end of each wire. Join a bulb and holder to each short wire on each side. The bulbs are now on different paths so if you take one bulb out the other stays lit. The current has another path to flow around the circuit. This is called a parallel circuit.

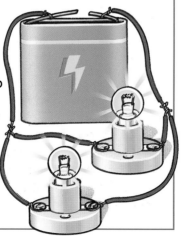

Conductors and insulators

Materials that allow electricity to flow through them are called conductors. Metals conduct electricity. Most electrical wire is made of copper which is a good conductor.

Insulators do not let electricity flow through them. Plastic is an insulator so most wire is covered in plastic to make it safe to handle.

Lamp

You will need: a matchbox; kitchen foil; four paper fasteners; a big safety pin; a 3.5v bulb; wire (see page 32); a small, square box with flip-top lid; cellophane; a paper clip; 4.5v battery; cardboard; ruler; scissors; glue stick.

Bulb holder

Push back prongs to touch the top of box.

1. Line the base and one end of the matchbox tray with foil. Push a paper fastener through the lined end. Ensure no foil sticks out over the top.

2. Poke a hole at one end of the top of the matchbox cover. Lay the hinge of the safety pin over the hole and push in a paper fastener.

Tip

Test that your matchbox bulb holder works before taping it to the box. Attach the wires to the battery terminals and if the bulb does not light up, check over the steps.

Put tray in as shown.

3. Make another hole in the top through the middle of the safety pin. Put the tray back in. Push the bulb into the hole - it must touch the foil inside.

4. Cut two long pieces of wire. Wind one piece around the fastener on the matchbox cover and the other around the fastener on the tray.

The box

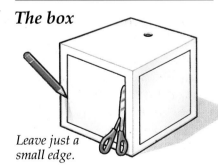

Leave just a small edge.

1. With a ruler, draw a square on each upright side of the box. Poke in scissors and cut them out. Make a hole in the lid big enough for two wires.

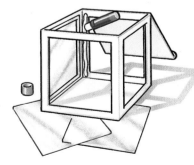

2. Cut cellophane squares to fit the windows you have made. Glue around the inside edges of the windows and stick the cellophane inside.

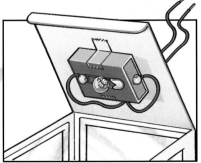

3. Push the free ends of the wires on the matchbox bulb holder up through the hole in the box lid. See if it works (Tip, above) then tape to lid.

Switch

Tape over the prongs at the back of the switch.

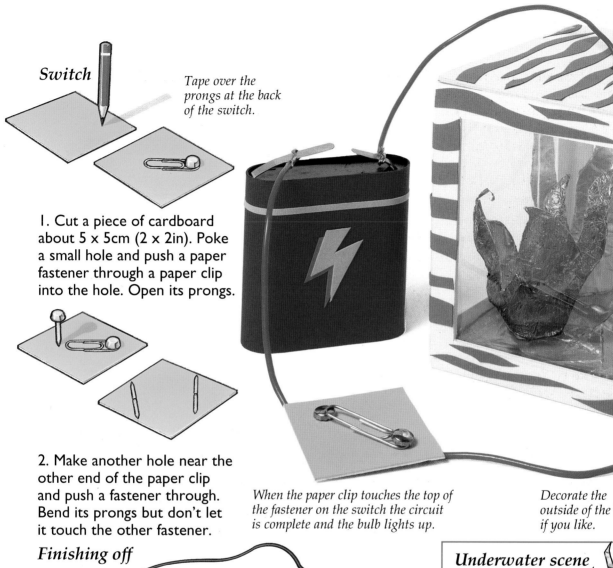

1. Cut a piece of cardboard about 5 x 5cm (2 x 2in). Poke a small hole and push a paper fastener through a paper clip into the hole. Open its prongs.

2. Make another hole near the other end of the paper clip and push a fastener through. Bend its prongs but don't let it touch the other fastener.

When the paper clip touches the top of the fastener on the switch the circuit is complete and the bulb lights up.

Decorate the outside of the box, if you like.

Finishing off

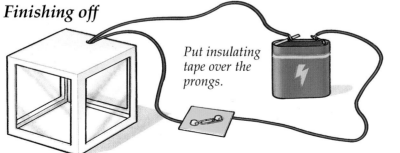

Put insulating tape over the prongs.

1. Close the lid and join the end of one wire to a battery terminal. Turn over the switch and join the other wire to one of the fasteners.

2. Cut a new piece of wire and wind it around the free fastener on the switch. Join the other end to the second battery terminal.

Underwater scene

Add some shells and make some sea plants out of foil for an underwater scene.

Cut some fish out of shiny paper. Hang them from the lid with thread.

13

Electric eel

You will need: four toilet roll cardboard tubes; scissors; tape; paint; three 1.5v bulbs; three bulb holders; a 9v battery; wire (see page 32 for advice).

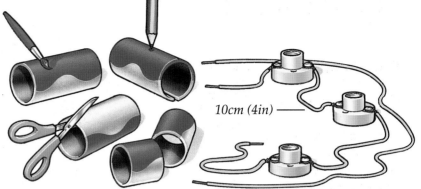

10cm (4in) ————

1. Paint the tubes. When dry, cut along the length of three of them. Make holes in the middle of these, opposite the cuts. Cut the fourth across the middle.

2. Wire up the bulb holders in a series, as shown (for help with making a series see page 10). Cut another piece of wire to match the length of the wired up bulb holders.

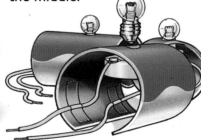

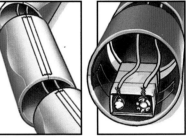

3. Push the bulbs through the holes in the three long toilet tubes. Screw them into the holders. Tape all the wires, including the unattached one, to the insides of the tubes.

4. Join the long tubes back together by taping along the cut you made in step 1. Tape the spare wires at one end to the battery. Then tape the battery inside a half tube.

The light will go on when the free ends of the wires touch.

Use your eel to test which materials conduct electricity. Touch both wires to different materials such as metal, plastic or foil and see if the bulbs light up.

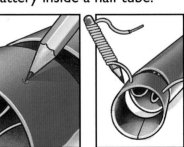

5. Make two small holes in the last half tube and push the other spare ends of the wires through. Wind them around a pencil to make them curly. Draw on eyes.

14

Pocket light

You will need: a small cardboard tube with a lid and a base (it should comfortably hold two 1.5v batteries laid end to end); a 2.5v bulb; two 1.5v batteries; foil; cardboard; some stiff paper.

Press the tabs together to make it light up.

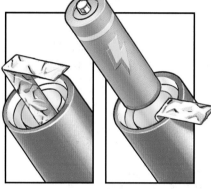

Cover or paint the tube if you like.

The rolled up paper stops the batteries from wobbling

1. Crumple some paper and push it into the end of the tube. This is to make sure that the batteries will almost reach the top of the tube when you put them in.

2. Roll up a piece of stiff paper and put it in the tube. Fold a piece of foil about 17cm (7in) long into a strip. Then fold up one end so that it makes a hook shape.

3. Put the strip of foil in the tube with the hooked end at the bottom and the other end dangling over the top edge. Now drop both batteries in, as shown.

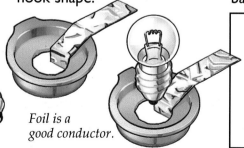

Foil is a good conductor.

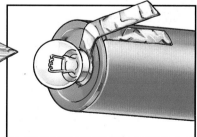

4. Ask an adult to make a hole in the lid of the tube with a sharp knife or hole punch. The hole should be large enough for the end of the bulb to go through.

5. Fold another piece of foil about 8cm (3in) long and press one end onto the edge of the hole in the lid, as shown. Push the bulb through the hole.

6. Put the lid on so the foil tabs are together but not touching. Press the top tab of foil onto the bottom to complete the circuit. The bulb will light up.

Buzzing treasure chest

You will need: a shoe box; thin cardboard; PVA (household) glue; tape; a small plate; a ballpoint pen; two brass paper fasteners; a steel paper clip; scissors; wire (see page 32 for advice); a 4.5v battery; a buzzer.

To line the treasure chest use bright fabric. Stick the edges of it to the box with double-sided tape or glue.

How it works

When you open the box the top paper fastener meets the paper clip. When these two metals touch, the circuit is completed, allowing the electricity to flow.

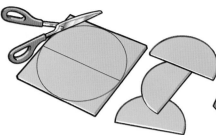

1. Draw and cut out two circles of cardboard. Use a small plate as a guide. Fold and cut them to make four half circles. Throw one away as you only need three.

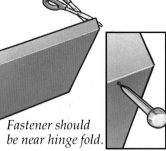

Fastener should be near hinge fold.

2. Snip the corners of one long side of the box lid. This will form a hinge. Make a hole with the ballpoint pen in one corner of the lid top, by the hinge. Push a paper fastener through.

If the buzzer doesn't work, swap around the wires on the battery.

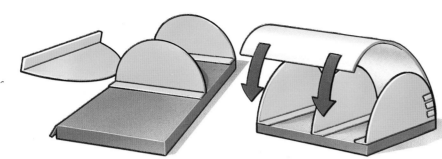
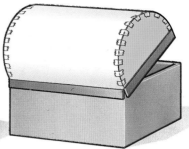

3. Fold up 1cm (½in) of the straight edge of each half circle to make tabs. Glue them onto the top of the lid. When dry, add tape to hold them more strongly.

4. Cut a piece of cardboard to fit over the half circles. Roll and unroll the cardboard first so that it curves over easily. Tape it to the half circles at either end.

5. Glue the back flap of the lid to the main part of the box to make a hinge. Tape along the hinge when the glue is dry. The lid will now open and shut easily.

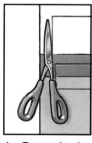
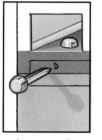

6. Cut a little window in the curved cardboard covering so you can see the first fastener. Make a hole just below it in the hinge. Push the second fastener through it.

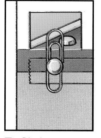
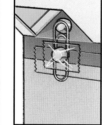

7. Slide a paper clip over the second fastener. Place it so that when you lift the lid of the box, the first paper fastener touches the paper clip. Tape it in position.

Decorating your box

Cover your box with papier mâché to strengthen it and hide any rough edges. To do this brush glue over the box and stick on strips of paper. Do it twice and let it dry. Then paint the chest.

Cover strips of cardboard with foil. Paint with a mix of black paint and glue. When dry, rub off as much paint as you can with a cloth. Now it looks like old silver. Glue them on the box as bands.

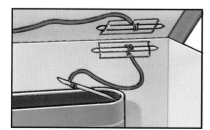

8. Inside the box, wind a wire around each fastener. Tape the wires to make sure they stay in place. Wind the end of one of the wires around a battery terminal.

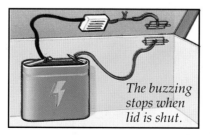

The buzzing stops when lid is shut.

9. Take the buzzer and attach one of its wires to the second wire. Attach the free buzzer wire to the other battery terminal. There should be a loud buzz.

Juggling clown

You will need: a cereal box; white and black paper; thin cardboard; three 1.5v bulbs; three bulb holders; wire (see page 32); a 1.5v battery in a battery holder; a metal paper clip; four paper fasteners; felt-tip pens; tape.

Before you start, dye one bulb red and one green with felt-tips.

1. Glue black paper onto the front of the box. Draw a clown on white paper, then paint and decorate it. Cut it out when dry and glue it onto the black paper.

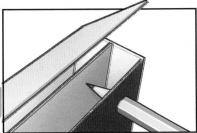

2. Cut a piece of cardboard to fit inside the box. Push a pencil through the black side to make holes for the juggling balls (light bulbs). Mark the cardboard through the holes.

Make sure that the wires reach the bottom of the box.

3. Take out the cardboard and tape bulb holders over the marks. Wire the holders using a separate wire for each connection. See page 10 for help wiring bulb holders.

4. Gather the wires from one side of each bulb holder and twist the ends together tightly. Now tape the three separate wires down onto the box.

5. Slide the wired up board into the cereal box. Now poke the bulbs through the holes you have made in the front of the box and screw them into the holders underneath.

Wiring up the switch

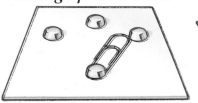

1. Push one paper fastener through a cardboard square. Slide a paper clip onto it. Add three more fasteners so that the other end of the paper clip can touch each one.

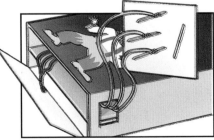

2. Cut a hole at the bottom of one side of the box. Poke the three separate wires out through it and wind each end around the legs of one of the three free fasteners.

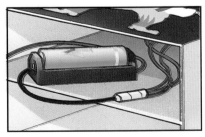

3. Inside the box attach the end of the three twisted wires to one end of the battery holder. Tape where they join to make sure they don't come apart.

How it works

As you move the paper clip around to touch each fastener on the switch, the individual circuit for each bulb is completed (see pages 10-11).

The bulbs light up in turn as their circuits are completed.

Stick some sequins and shiny paper onto your clown.

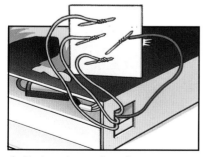

4. Poke the other battery holder wire through the hole in the box. Wind the end of the wire around the back of the paper fastener with the paper clip on the switch.

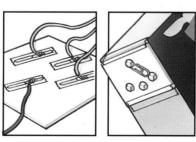

5. Tape over all the connections and then tape the switch to the side of the box. Tape up the top and bottom of the box with the battery inside.

Tip

Make sure that when you touch the fasteners with the paper clip they light up in the right order so that the clown looks as though he is juggling. If they don't light up in turn, swap around the wires on the three free fasteners of the switch.

19

Lighting-up T-shirt

You will need: 2 LEDs; wire (see page 32 for advice about wire); T-shirt; 4.5v battery; insulating tape; silver foil; squeeze-on fabric paint; cardboard; chalk; two metal paper clips.

LED stands for light-emitting diode. LEDs are tiny, so come in handy for some jobs. You must disconnect the wires and take them out when you wash the T-shirt.

1. Wash your T-shirt first if it is new. This gets rid of any coating which stops paint from being absorbed. Iron the shirt and put cardboard inside to stretch it flat.

2. Draw a spider design like this in chalk. You can dust it off and start again if you are not happy with it. Now go over the design with fabric paint. Let it dry.

 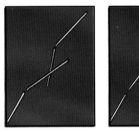

3. Take out the cardboard. Push the legs of the LEDs to the inside of the shirt for the spider's eyes. Make sure the short (-) leg of one LED is next to the long (+) leg of the other.

4. Bend the legs back so that the LEDs are firmly attached to the T-shirt. Then twist together the long (+) and short (-) leg which are nearest each other.

Make sure the wires are long enough to reach below the bottom of your shirt.

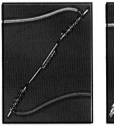  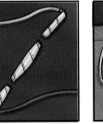 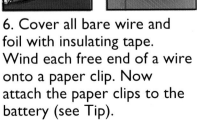

5. Wind a wire around the free long (+) leg. Wind another around the free short (-) leg. Wrap foil around all the connections, this helps conduct the electricity.

6. Cover all bare wire and foil with insulating tape. Wind each free end of a wire onto a paper clip. Now attach the paper clips to the battery (see Tip).

Put the battery in a pocket.

Baseball cap

Decorate a hat and add LEDs. The wires should be long enough for you to put the battery in a pocket.

Bow-tie

Make a paper bow-tie and attach flashing LEDs.

Tip

LEDs only let electricity flow one way. This means that the wire from the short negative leg must go to the negative (-) battery terminal and the wire from the long positive leg must go to the positive (+) terminal.

If the LEDs don't light up, the paper clips might be attached to the wrong terminals. Switch them around and see.

You can also buy flashing LEDs.

Whizzing plane

You will need: a 3v motor; a propeller measuring 12cm (5in) from tip to tip (buy these in model or hobby stores); a 1.5v battery and holder; thin cardboard; string; a round hook; tape; a rubber band; a length of square dowel 30cm (1ft) long (you can buy this quite cheaply in hardware stores). Ask an adult to cut the dowel to the right size.

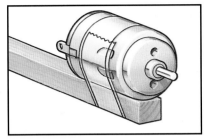

1. Tape the motor on top of one end of the dowel, as shown. Make sure it doesn't wobble around.

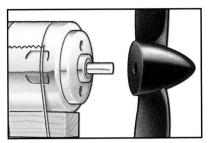

2. Poke the prong on the front of the motor firmly into the hole in the back of the propeller.

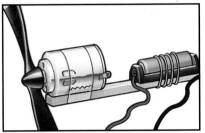

3. Put your battery into the battery holder and then attach it to the dowel with a rubber band.

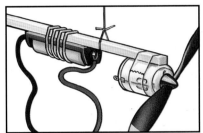

4. Balance the plane by tying string between the battery and motor. Move the string until the plane hangs level.

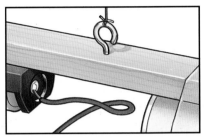

5. Where it hangs level, mark the place. Then screw in the hook. Tie about 1 metre (3ft) of string, to the hook.

The plane's body

You can use glue if you like but ask an adult for help.

Glue both halves of the plane's body to the dowel, one on each side.

Trace the templates for the body and wings on page 24 onto thin, bright cardboard. Cut them out. Tape both halves of the plane's body along the dowel. The slits for the wings should be below the battery. Now slide the wings through the slits.

Trace lightning shapes from templates onto bright paper. Cut out and glue on.

Glue on a cockpit cut from white paper.

This plane was made from thin, plastic packaging, not cardboard. It works just the same.

WARNING: THIS PLANE'S WHIZZING PROPELLER COULD HURT YOU. NEVER FLY IT NEAR PEOPLE.

Flying the plane

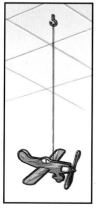

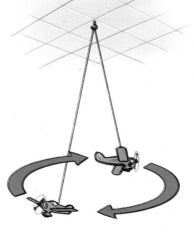

Ask permission to attach a hook firmly to the ceiling. Tie the free end of the string to it. Wind the end of each battery wire to a prong on the motor to make the propeller turn. Push the plane to start it whizzing around.

Checklist

Make sure that the propeller is turning the right way. To test this, attach a strip of paper to a pencil. Hold it by the body.

If the paper blows in the direction of the propeller rather than the tail, switch the wires on the motor.

23

Tracing the plane

1. Lay a sheet of tracing paper over the template. Attach it with paper clips to keep it steady.

2. Trace all the lines (do two fuselages). Turn the tracing over. Scribble soft pencil over the outlines.

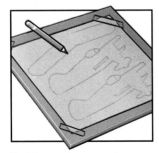

3. Turn the tracing back over and lay it onto cardboard. Pencil over the lines and the shape will appear.

24

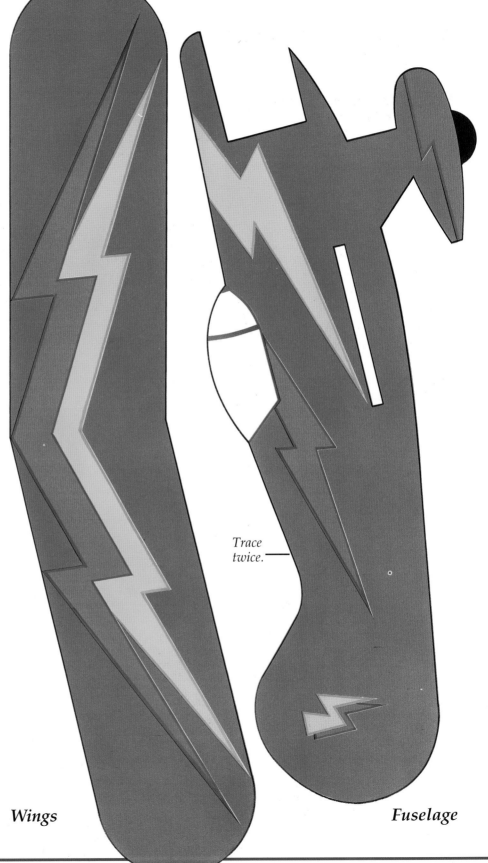

Trace twice.

Wings

Fuselage

Making an electromagnet

You will need: an iron bolt or nail; sandpaper; some glazed copper wire; tape; 4.5v battery.

For a switch you need: a piece of cardboard; 2 paper fasteners; wire; paper clip.

Electromagnetism

Electricity can turn iron or steel into a magnet. You put an iron or steel rod through a coil of wire. When you pass current through the wire, the rod becomes a magnet. If you switch the current off, it stops being magnetic. The process, which was discovered in the last century, is called electromagnetism and it is used in many modern machines, such as electromagnetic cranes (see page 26).

1. Scrape about 2cm (1in) of varnish off both ends of the glazed copper wire with a piece of sandpaper. You need to do this carefully or your electromagnet will not work.

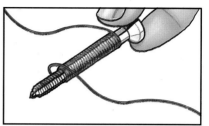

2. Hold one end of the wire against the bolt or the nail and wind the wire around and around until you reach the end. Keep the coils very close together.

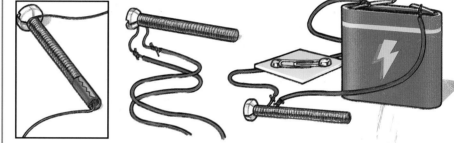

3. At the point of the nail put tape on the wire and wind it back up to the beginning. Cut two pieces of ordinary wire and join one end of each to the copper wires.

4. Make a switch (see page 11). Join one switch wire to the battery and the second to an electromagnet wire. Join the free electromagnet wire to the second battery terminal.

Switch on the electromagnet and try picking up a few metal paper clips or pins. Watch what happens when you switch the current off.

The more turns of wire on the coil, the stronger the magnet.

Use ordinary, plastic-coated wire (see page 32) if you can't find glazed copper wire.

25

Electromagnet crane

For the crane you will need: a strong cardboard box, about 10cm (5in) square; stiff cardboard; a cotton reel (US thread spool); pencils; piece of string 30cm (12in) long; three paper clips; an electromagnet (see page 25); 4.5v battery; three paper fasteners; tape; scissors; wire (see page 32 for advice).

For the base: a box about 15 x 10cm (6 x 5in); 2 toilet paper tubes; corrugated cardboard; glue; black paint.

The driver's cab will swivel around.

Making the crane

1. Cut off the top of the box. Then cut two strips of cardboard the same length. Make slits in one side of the box, as shown, for the strips to slot through.

Wiring up

1. Tie the electromagnet to the end of the string. Coil its wires around a pencil. Poke two holes in the front of the box with a sharp pencil and feed the wires through.

Pick iron or steel objects up, move the crane around, then drop them by turning off the current.

Moving things like this, with a big electromagnetic crane is very useful in real life.

Bend ends of paper clip back to hold.

2. Slot strips in. Make holes in box and strips. Add paper fasteners. Make holes at the far end of each strip, insert a cotton reel and push through a straightened paper clip.

3. Bend a paper clip for a handle. Tape it to the end of a pencil. Make two holes with a pencil point in the sides of the box behind the strips and push the pencil through.

4. Put one end of the piece of string on the middle of the pencil and hold it in place with sticky tape. Run the string over the cotton reel and let it hang.

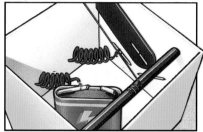

2. Push a paper fastener through the side of the box and open its prongs. Push a second fastener through a paper clip and into the box, near the first fastener.

3. Wind one of the wires from the electromagnet around one paper fastener. Attach the other wire from the electromagnet to the battery terminal.

4. Cut a new piece of wire. Wind one end of it around the second paper fastener. Then attach the other end of it to the second battery terminal.

The base

Put it together

Corrugated cardboard

I. Cut the toilet tubes in half to make four wheels and then stick them onto the base box, as shown here. Wait for the glue to dry and then paint the box and wheels.

2. Cut strips of corrugated cardboard (chocolate box packaging is good for this) to fit over the wheels. Curve the strips around the wheels and tape the ends.

Poke a paper fastener into the bottom of the wired-up box and through a piece of corrugated cardboard. Push the fastener into the top of the base and open the prongs.

27

Spooky house

For the house you will need: a big cardboard box; glue stick; orange cellophane; white paint or chalk; several sheets of black paper.

There's lots to do to make this house on the next four pages, but it's well worth it. Before you start, turn the box onto a long side and glue black paper to all the sides inside. Add brick markings with white paint or chalk.

Witch and cat

You will need: black stiff paper; an oblong box large enough to fit over the hole in the back of the box; a 1.5v bulb; 1.5v bulb in a battery holder; wire; scissors; tape; paper fasteners; paper clip.

Witch and cat shape

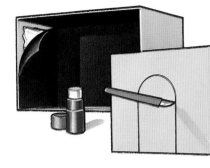

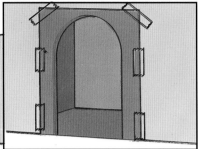

1. Cut a door shape in the back of the box, about 23 x 13cm (9in x 5in). A craft knife is best for this. Ask an adult to help with sharp knives.

2. Cut a rectangle of orange cellophane (you could also use orange tissue paper) slightly larger than the door. Tape it over the door at the back.

1. Draw and cut out a witch and cat from stiff, black paper. You could copy the shape below. The witch and cat should fill most of the door hole in the back.

2. With scissors, cut off one big side of the oblong box. Turn it over and make a hole near one end of the back with a pencil. Push the bulb base through from the front.

3. Screw the bulb into a bulb holder and wire up the bulb holder into a circuit with the battery. Add a switch (see pages 10-11 for how to do all of this).

4. Tape the witch and cat onto the cellophane in the house doorway from behind. Tape the open side of the oblong box to the big box so the bulb is behind the witch.

Coffin

You will need: a box about 16 x 8cm (6 x 3in), cut around three sides near the top to make a lifting lid; white tissue paper; paint; 1.5v bulb and holder; wire; 1.5v battery and holder; 2 small magnets; glue; thread.

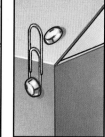

1. In a corner, by the hinge, push a paper fastener into the back of the box and one into the lid. Slide a paper clip over the bottom one so it touches the other when the lid is up.

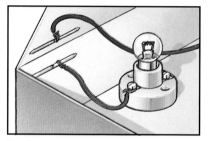

2. Cut two pieces of wire. Wind one end of each around one leg of each fastener. Attach the free end of one wire to a bulb holder screw.

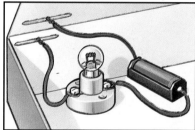

3. Join the second free end to one of the battery holder wires. Wind the second battery wire to the bulb holder. Bulb lights up when the lid is open (see page 16).

Lay skeleton in coffin and glue hand to inside of lid.

4. Put a layer of cellophane in the coffin. Draw a skeleton (see right) on white paper and cut out.

CONTINUES ON NEXT PAGE.

Skull

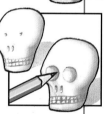

To make the skull roll a ball of self-hardening clay. Press in the sides to make a skull shape. With a pencil point mark eyes, nose and teeth. Join two red LEDs and wire them as described on page 20. Push a pencil point right through the eyes to make holes for the LEDs. Poke in the LEDs from the back. Let the clay harden.

29

Spider

You will need: four bright pipe cleaners; 2 LEDs (see page 20); 4.5v battery; paper clip; paper fastener; wire; tape.

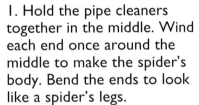

1. Hold the pipe cleaners together in the middle. Wind each end once around the middle to make the spider's body. Bend the ends to look like a spider's legs.

2. Link the LEDs by one short and one long leg and tape. Tape around the tops of the free legs. Push the LED prongs into the spider's body. See page 20 for how to use LEDs.

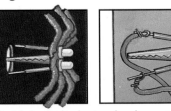

3. Make a hole in the box to push the LED legs through. Attach a wire to each of the two free LED legs. Attach the wires to a battery and add a switch (see page 10-11).

30

Make a hole in the bottom of the box and feed the coffin wires through.

Paint a picture of a person or cut one from a magazine. Cut the eyes out and stick green cellophane over the holes at the back.

Draw some chalk cobwebs on black paper, cut out and and stick them to the walls.

Make a hole for the wires of the skull's LEDs in the base of the box. Feed the wires through the hole so all you can see is the skull in the box. Take the wires behind the box and attach to the battery there.

Shimmering ghost

You will need: magnets; self-adhesive tabs; white cardboard; tape; white tissue paper; a pipe cleaner; needle and fine thread.

1. Draw a ghost shape on white cardboard and cut out. Glue one side and stick it to a larger piece of white tissue. Cut the tissue all around the ghost shape, but a bit bigger.

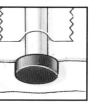

2. Tape a straw to the back of the ghost. The end should stick below the cardboard a bit. Stick a self-adhesive tab to the end of the straw and add a magnet, behind the tissue.

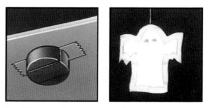

3. Tape the second magnet to bottom of the box (make sure the poles push away as shown on pages 6-7). Hang the ghost in the box so that it hovers over the magnet.

31

Things you need to know

Before you start any of the projects in this book, it's a good idea to gather together all the things you need. For many of them you will need scissors, glue, pencils and a ruler. You can buy wire, bulbs, bulb holders, batteries, battery holders, insulating tape, LEDs and buzzers from electrical stores. Large toy stores and some hardware stores sell magnets.

Magnets

Magnets come in all sorts of sizes and shapes. You can get small round ones which are often used for refrigerator magnets, bar magnets, round ones with holes in the middle and horseshoe shaped ones. Some magnets are more powerful than others. You can test your magnet's strength by seeing how close it needs to be to attract something metal, such as a paper clip. The closer it needs to be to the metal, the weaker the magnet.

Batteries

The amount of energy a battery stores is measured in volts. This is usually shortened to "v". On each battery there is a number, such as 1.5v or 4.5v, which tells you how much electrical energy is stored in that battery. Do not use a more powerful battery than you need. In this book it tells you which type of battery to use for each project. Only use the type suggested. Never use the mains electricity for any experiments as it is very dangerous.

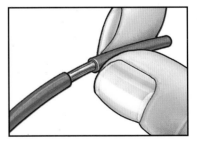

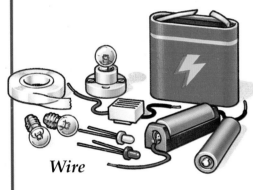

Wire

For all the projects in this book you can use miniature stranded wire. This consists of lots of fine strands and is easy to bend. You can use other fine wires with single strand cores, but they are not so flexible. Most wire is insulated which means it has a covering - usually plastic - which does not let electricity flow through it. To prepare a wire for a circuit you must strip the ends (see right).

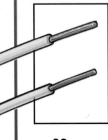

Stripping wires

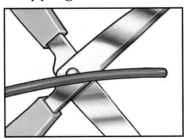

To strip the ends, you need to take off about 3cm (1½in) of plastic to leave bare wire at the end. Open your scissors wide and very gently cut the plastic all around the wire. Once

you have cut all the plastic around the wire, gently slide off the cut piece. If the wire is made up of strands, twist them together. Be careful with the single strand kind as the wire can be sharp.